ARDMORE ELEMENTARY LIBRARY
BELLEVUE, WASHINGTON

Chinook!

by MICHAEL O. TUNNELL

pictures by BARRY ROOT

TAMBOURINE BOOKS  NEW YORK

Text copyright © 1993 by Michael O. Tunnell

Illustrations copyright © 1993 by Barrett V. Root

All rights reserved. No part of this book may be reproduced
or utilized in any form or by any means, electronic or
mechanical, including photocopying, recording, or by any
information storage or retrieval system, without permission in
writing from the Publisher. Inquiries should be addressed to
Tambourine Books, a division of William Morrow & Company, Inc.,
1350 Avenue of the Americas, New York, New York 10019.
Printed in Singapore.

Library of Congress Cataloging in Publication Data
Tunnell, Michael O. Chinook/by Michael O. Tunnell; illustrated by Barry
Root. p. cm.—summary: Mr. Andy tells Thad and Annie some tales about
the spectacular effects of chinooks, hot winter winds that suddenly
spring up and cause dramatic changes in the temperature.
[1. Winds—Fiction. 2. Tall tales.] I. Root, Barry, ill. II. Title.
PZ7.T825Ch 1993 [E]—dc20 92-12711 CIP AC
ISBN 0-688-10869-5.—ISBN 0-688-10870-9 (library ed.)
10 9 8 7 6 5 4 3 2 1
First edition

To Nanny and Papa—
who raised me in Chinook country M.O.T.

To Tom, Peggy, and Gwynn   B.R.

Annie and I pushed through the spruce woods, toting our ice skates and wading through knee-deep snow. We'd just moved from the East, so we'd never been to the lake. But the Ramseys from down the road said it was a fine place to skate because roaring winds swept the ice clean.

As we neared the lake, Annie ran ahead while I stopped to pull my toque from a low-hanging branch. "Thad," she whispered back to me, "look at this!"

A rowboat sat on the ice, a hundred yards from shore. Smoke rose lazily from one end and a dark lump was piled at the other.

We shucked our boots, pulled on our skates, and were soon rattling across the ice. As we came near the boat, I pointed to a small potbellied stove topped with a whistling tea kettle. But Annie was more interested in the dark lump. From this pile of blankets and coats and hats and scarves, a fishing rod stuck out like a flagpole, its line dangling through a jagged hole in the ice.

Annie's eyes fastened on the lump and I knew what she was thinking.
But before she could grab the first blanket, an old man exploded from the
heap, waving his arms wildly.

"Heavenly days! What are you young 'uns doing this far from shore?
Get in the boat! Hurry, I say!" he yelled, sounding so frantic Annie and I
climbed aboard.

"Ah, there. That's better," he wheezed, leaning heavily against the
boat. "Never safe, you know. Not here on Lake Turnabout. McFadden's the
name, Andrew Delaney McFadden. Call me Andy." He raised a bushy gray
eyebrow. "Cup of tea?"

A moment later, Andy handed us steaming mugs of tea. "I figure you're the folks from out East who bought old Harvey's place," he said, offering us sugar cubes and a tin of milk. Annie and I both nodded.

"Pardon me, Mr. Andy," I asked between sips. "Why are you ice fishing in a rowboat?"

"Ah," Andy sighed, staring at the Rocky Mountains to the west. "Chinooks, my boy. Chinooks. A granddaddy chinook can be near as dangerous as an earthquake or a twister.

"You Easterners don't know about such things, I reckon. A chinook is wind. But not just any old wind, mind you. It comes unexpected in the coldest part of winter. Regular ones come every year—warm as a spring day, causing quite a thaw. But granddaddy chinooks are hot as breath from a blast furnace. The Indians say granddaddies come every fifty years.

"I remember my first granddaddy, the winter of eighteen hundred and eighty-eight. There wasn't much snow that year, but it was as cold as a snake's kiss. I was out on the lake ice fishing, sitting just about where we are right now. I heard what sounded like the roar of a locomotive and looked up to see Horace McRae barreling down that hill right over there in his sleigh. He was whipping his horses and yelling to beat all. I stood up for a better look and saw that the front of his sled runners were in the snow but the back of the runners were sinking in mud! Yes sir, that granddaddy could melt snow faster than those horses could run.

"Well, I threw my fishing gear aside and began to run for the opposite shore. I peered over my shoulder and saw Horace bogged down, his horses collapsed in the mud. Then I lost sight of him as steam commenced to rise from the lake. The chinook had already started to take the ice and I could hear it just a sizzlin'. Sure I'd never make it, I kicked off my boots, stripped off my coat, and kept running barefoot across the ice. I was still fifty yards from solid ground when the chinook caught me. That wind was blistering hot, fairly roasting me. Then I dropped into the water.

"I bobbed in old Lake Turnabout and watched the ice disappear, slicker and faster than a travellin' magic man can make a silver dollar vanish right afore your eyes. Well, the water was so hot and I was so tuckered out that I barely made it to shore alive. That's why I drag this boat out here every time I go ice fishing, 'cause you can't outrun a granddaddy.

"As it turned out, that chinook was just the beginning of a string of granddaddies that stretched over five years. The next winter the snow was up above the rooftops by January, and it was teeth rattlin' cold. Why, I had to dig a tunnel from my cabin to the barn and fashion a snow ramp from the barn door up to the surface. I'd drive my team and sleigh right up that ramp to the top of all that snow that fierce winds had packed as hard as stone.

"I was up on the snow heading to Sunday meetings when granddaddy number two blew in. I felt a change in the icy air and looked behind me to see a cloud of hissing, snorting steam rolling my way. I whipped my horses, trying to outrun it, but was soon sucked inside that boiling, dripping cloud. The sleigh sloshed back and forth like it was sinking in Lake Turnabout; then suddenly the sky cleared. My sleigh was sitting on ground as parched and cracked as if we'd had a summer-long drought. The horses were lying on their sides, half drowned, half cooked.

"Pulling off my heavy clothes, I stumbled toward the church. Now, the snow had been so deep that we'd used the steeple as a hitching post for our horses. What a shock to see horses dangling from the steeple by their reins and sleighs dangling from the horses. Everyone was running around trying to figure out how to get them down without dropping the animals and breaking the sleighs to splinters. What a sight!

"After that day, folks just kept themselves chinook prepared. Why, Sally McRae always took a summer dress and sunbonnet whenever she and Horace went visiting in the winter—just in case a chinook came along and folks got a picnic together. And sleighs were built with wheels that could be lowered into place—no more being stranded on dry ground. In fact, some folks started building sleighs that were watertight like a boat.

"After all this, I figured we'd seen everything," said Andy, shaking his head slowly. "But we were still in for a mighty big surprise. Got a double-barreled shot the third winter. Two granddaddy chinooks within days of one another. The first one melted all the snow and ice; the flood water was six feet deep. You should have seen folks floating in their new boat-sleighs, horses barely able to keep their noses above water.

"The second chinook dried up the floods, but it didn't stop there! No sir, it dried up all the water in the streams and most of it in the lakes, too. We gathered up all the trout flopping in the dry stream beds and smoked the whole lot. We had dried fish to last for years.

"And both those chinooks plumb fooled all the trees—confused 'em so that they budded and leaved in one day. And the apple trees bore fruit the next day. Yes sir, what great apple pies we had that winter. And we got a whole new crop again when autumn rolled around.

"Our poor old apple trees were fooled again a year later when a real ripsnortin' granddaddy blasted in and caused the biggest apple crop ever seen hereabouts. Then the fifth winter I even had tomatoes in February, all from seeds that had fallen into the ground the summer before."

"And what about the year after that, Mr. Andy, sir?" I asked.

"Only a regular chinook, boy. Only regular ones ever since. But it's been fifty years, so it's time again. You see why I wanted you to get into the boat?"

"But it's time for us to get home," Annie said. "How will we get back?"

Andy rubbed his chin, then began to chuckle. "Guess I worry a mite too much. You two skate on over to the bank. If a granddaddy comes, I'll row like the dickens and pick you out of the water."

We thanked Andrew McFadden for the tea and waved to him, off and on, all the way back to the shore. We traded skates for snowboots and then turned to look one more time at Andy's boat.

But that side of Lake Turnabout was covered with thick, boiling fog. It was rolling toward us with a deep rumble.

I looked at Annie and laughed. "How about a swim this afternoon?"